What Can I Bee?
I Could Bee a
Teacher!

Written by
Amy Culliford

Illustrated by
John Joseph

A Blossoms Beginning Readers Book

CRABTREE
Publishing Company
www.crabtreebooks.com

Level 1 Early Emergent Readers Grades PK-K

Books at this level have strong picture support with carefully controlled text and repetitive patterns. They feature a limited number of words on each page and large, easy-to-read print.

Level 2 Emergent Readers Grade 1

Books at this level have a more complex sentence structure and more lines of text per page. They depend less on repetitive patterns and pictures. Familiar topics are explored, but with greater depth.

Level 3 Early Readers Grade 2

Books at this level are carefully developed to tell a great story, but in a format that children are able to read and enjoy by themselves. They feature familiar vocabulary and appealing illustrations.

Level 4 Fluent Readers Grade 3

Books at this level have more text and use challenging vocabulary. They explore less familiar topics and continue to help refine and strengthen reading skills to get ready for chapter books.

School-to-Home Support for Caregivers and Teachers

This book helps children grow by letting them practice reading. Here are a few guiding questions to help the reader with building his or her comprehension skills. Possible answers appear here in red.

Before Reading:

• What do I think this story will be about?
  • *I think this story will be about a bee who wants to be a teacher.*
  • *I think this story will be about what a teacher does.*

During Reading:

• Pause and look at the words and pictures. Why did the character do that?
  • *I think the bee is writing on a chalkboard so that all of the students can see.*
  • *I think the bee has a lot of books because he needs to read about all the subjects he teaches.*

After Reading:

• Describe your favorite part of the story.
  • *My favorite part was when the bee was standing in front of the school and waving to everyone.*

What could I be?

3

I could be a teacher!

5

I could go to school.

I could have lots
of books.

I could sit at a desk.

I could use a chalkboard.

13

WRITING PROMPTS

Possible answers appear here in red.

1. **Write a different ending to the story.**

The bee decided to teach a science class, and tried a new experiment!

2. **Choose a character and write the story from that character's point of view.**

The new student in class was excited to have a brand new teacher!

3. **Write about a similar situation that you experienced.**

This reminds me of when my new teacher brought in a stack of books and started a book club!

ABOUT THE AUTHOR

Amy Culliford has been involved in the arts her entire life. After completing a Bachelor of Fine Arts degree at the University of Victoria, she worked for several years as a drama teacher in classrooms and after school programs. Presently, Amy works for a professional opera company by day, writes children's books by night, and performs as a princess at children's birthday parties on weekends. If she has any spare time, she likes to spend it planning her next trip to Disneyland!

ABOUT THE ILLUSTRATOR

John Joseph's passion for art appeared at an early age, while living in Orlando, Florida. As a young boy, he was inspired by his many trips to visit the animation studios just down the road, at the happiest place on Earth. It was very rare that you would spot him without a pencil and sketchbook, creating stories and drawing away.

John Joseph's love of art continued through school, and he went on to get an art education degree from Colorado State University and a masters degree from Lesley University. You could say that John has never really left school, as he graduated and went straight back to elementary school to teach visual arts. He is constantly inspired by the imagination of his students, and often includes them in his stories and illustrations.

What Can I Bee?

I Could Bee a Teacher!

Written by: Amy Culliford

Illustrations by: John Joseph

Art direction and layout by:

Under the Oaks Media

Series Development: James Earley

Proofreader: Kathy Middleton

Educational Consultant:

Marie Lemke M.Ed.

Print and production coordinator:

Katherine Berti

Library and Archives Canada Cataloguing in Publication

Title: I could bee a teacher! / written by Amy Culliford ; illustrated by John Joseph.
Names: Culliford, Amy, 1992- author. | Joseph, John, 1985- illustrator.
Description: Series statement: What can I bee? | "A blossoms beginning readers book".
Identifiers: Canadiana (print) 20210225939 | Canadiana (ebook) 20210225947 | ISBN 9781427153753 (hardcover) | ISBN 9781427153814 (softcover) | ISBN 9781427153876 (HTML) | ISBN 9781427153937 (EPUB) | ISBN 9781427153999 (read-along ebook)
Subjects: LCSH: Readers (Primary) | LCSH: Teachers—Juvenile literature. | LCSH: Teaching—Juvenile literature. | LCGFT: Readers (Publications)
Classification: LCC PE1119.2 .C842 2022 | DDC j428.6—dc23

Library of Congress Cataloging-in-Publication Data

Names: Culliford, Amy, 1992- author. | Joseph, John, 1985- illustrator.
Title: I could bee a teacher! / written by Amy Culliford ; illustrated by John Joseph.
Description: New York, NY : Crabtree Publishing Company, [2022] | Series: What can I bee?
Identifiers: LCCN 2021023545 (print) | LCCN 2021023546 (ebook) | ISBN 9781427153753 (hardcover) | ISBN 9781427153814 (paperback) | ISBN 9781427153876 (ebook) | ISBN 9781427153937 (epub) | ISBN 9781427153999
Subjects: LCSH: Readers (Primary) | Teachers--Juvenile fiction. | LCGFT: Readers (Publications) | Picture books.
Classification: LCC PE1119.2 .C8495 2022 (print) | LCC PE1119.2 (ebook) | DDC 428.6/2--dc23
LC record available at https://lccn.loc.gov/2021023545

Crabtree Publishing Company

www.crabtreebooks.com   1-800-387-7650

Printed in the U.S.A./072021/CG20210514

Published in the United States
Crabtree Publishing
347 Fifth Avenue, Suite 1402-145
New York, NY, 10016

Published in Canada
Crabtree Publishing
616 Welland Ave.
St. Catharines, ON, L2M 5V6